The Fishing Story

By Duane "Red" Clasen
& Joe Hinshaw

A Mouse Gate Adventure

Mouse Gate Press
1103 Middlecreek
Friendswood,   Texas   77546
281-992-3131 TL
www.totalrecallpress.com

ISBN: 978-1-64883-0464
UPC: 6-43977-40464-0
Library of Congress Control Number: 2020942581
Printed in the United States of America with simultaneous
printings in Australia, Canada, and United Kingdom.

FIRST EDITION
1   2   3   4   5   6   7   8   9   10

To my Grandson's Bradley
Hayward Hauser II (B2HSquared)
and Barrett Brahm Hauser (2BH1)

For providing the time, opportunity
and the understanding to let an old
man pursue his dreams and to
support him in his efforts providing
him with the muse and imagination
for this book.

To all of the characters in the book
who represent real life people who
experienced the basic story with
Red Clasen

Author Joe Hinshaw

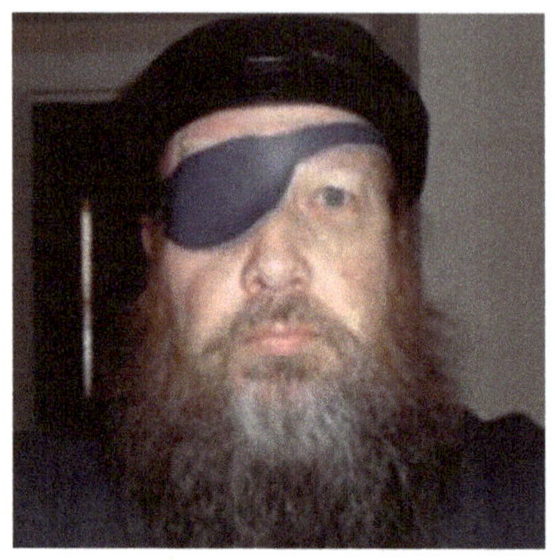

Joe Hinshaw grew up in Indianapolis Indiana. He had his taste of farm life working on farms in the suburbs during his teen years. Later he moved to the country and lived there several years. He could see first-hand the difficulties of the small family farms and watched them disappear due to the economy, development and government blunders. It struck home at the first of the Farm Aid concerts with major entertainers educating the public of the plight of the farmer. Some of those were Willie Nelson, Neil Young, John Mellencamp and many others.

Duane "Red Clasen

Duane "Red Clasen's grew up in Northern Iowa and the experience and story line are his own. This story comes from his childhood and for the most part are actual events in his life. There is an element of fiction to bring the story together to add some interest and some elements that hopes to bring the plight of the farmers to the generation that this book is intended to target. It is our hope that educating young men and women of these issues that they might be the leaders of tomorrow that will address these issues.

Acknowledgement:

I would like to acknowledge my Godmother Florence Maxwell for contributing and supporting me as a writer when I was about 12 years old. She was a school teacher and helped me edit my first book at that age. It also gave me the internal drive to revisit my writing passion as life experiences allowed this pursuit. Also my parents, This section could not be complete without acknowledging my publisher, Bruce Moran of Total Recall Publications and all of those he had reading and critiquing the content. It is a difficult thing for a new writer to stay within their own parameters and age groups and an even more difficult thing for someone to tell you that you missed your targets in some areas. Thank you for getting me on track.

The Fishing Story

Growing up in rural northern Iowa in the early 1960s was a rare slice of America. It was not like growing up in a city and therefore it provided its own traditions, culture, history and experiences. The legacy of fishing was deeply embedded in every man and boy in this sparsely populated area of our country. This is not to say that fishing was not an important part of cultures all over the world but in my small world, as a boy eager to join the march into manhood, it was a major milestone in my life.

For years I would sit on the fringes of conversations where old men boasted of their fishing prowess and successes. The older boys had their own area in the bait store for this sort of storytelling also. In fact there were sections for each age group that had finished their first solo fishing trip. In each story the number of catches and the size of the fish seemed to grow. I once reckoned if one of the sessions lasted too long that the sheer weight of all these fish would end up sinking the boat they were in. I thought that comparably a whale would look like a minnow compared to the fish that was claimed to have been caught. Although there were many questionable stories traded, it was fishing etiquette to never question the validity of one's story even if you were present and knew it to be a whopper.

It was a normal part of life to go out fishing with your father, grandfather or in my case my uncle. This was an honor and a time of pride in early life. This ritual resembled the stories I had heard of young Indian braves who were taught their hunting skills as soon as they could walk. These skills were practiced and honed until the brave reached the age of eleven or twelve years. At that time the brave would be sent on his own into the woods to make his first kill and show his worth to the tribe. Sadly, if he failed he was cast from the tribe to live on his own or given unmanly tasks to do the rest of his life after failing his test. In Iowan culture we had much the same test of manhood but without the dire consequences.

My eleventh birthday was approaching on June 20, 1968. I was coming to my own crossroads. It did not sneak up on me. I had prepared over many years. I was being taught the finer points of fishing by my uncle and absorbing every story of the older boys and old men. I had saved my money and planned well. I purchased my fishing rod first. This allowed me to learn to cast and practice this skill with lead weights tied to the line.

First, I would cast for distance. I would then cast for accuracy by trying to land the weights in our trashcans at various distances. I became very good at both skills. Next I found a small tackle box and set about loading it with hooks, sinkers, bobbers and extra line. I took careful notes while listening to the fishing stories and acquired every lure I could find that these fishing pros had discussed. I got up early and dug all day and past dark to capture a large supply of worms, crickets and assorted bugs that could become my secret weapon of baits in fishdom. Some of these worms, bugs and crickets would be sold to the bait store or traded to them for additional fishing gear for my tackle box.

While caught up in this rush towards manhood I never once sat down to consider the actual event, as it would play out. Through all of the hours working to earn money for fishing gear practicing my casting and accumulating all of the newest and most successful lures the only image that came to my mind was of the big parade and all the newspaper headlines around the world about the size and amount of fish I would likely catch. There was no possibility of failure. I had prepared and learned. I had the best equipment and I was a good fisherman for my age. I knew that my uncle and his fishing buddies never really listened to my ideas. I knew they were good ideas and just waiting to be proven. Now, unfettered by the interference of elders, I would become the greatest fisherman in the entire world. I would be legendary in fact. I would probably be asked to have my own fishing show on the TV. There I would help all the lesser fishermen and kids learn how to catch fish. I could only show them so much though. After all, if I told them my best ideas I would no longer be the best. Fishing is a thinking man's game or at least I heard it was from all the fish stories. That one secret place, secret bait or the psychic ability to read fish's minds had to be kept to oneself. This I intended to do like all great fishermen. On my TV show I would teach the basics so people could catch fish but not be a challenge to me. Of course I would also win most of the tournaments once my secrets were turned loose on the fishing world and would earn millions of dollars and get free gear and boats. What I life I will have then. These thoughts were continually in my mind. The only thing holding me back was reaching my eleventh birthday.

As the days went by they passed slower and slower. The fishing trips with my uncle had lost their excitement. This did not go unnoticed but the subject was never discussed. I did not use my special baits or secrets because I would need them for the big day. I caught my share of fish and with each one, no matter how small, my uncle and the other men would slap me on the back and make a big show of it. They did not do this for each other. In fact, a small fish would cause much ridicule and set off loud jokes where there was much swearing and jawing at each other. I made a mental note to learn how to swear properly. I knew they could bleep it from my TV show anyway.

As the day approached, I had spent much time at the library reading fishing magazines and books that taught how to fish in all kinds of weather. They talked about the colors and types of lures and what conditions and what types of fish you were most likely to have success with each one of them. It talked about live bait like worms and bugs. There were articles about self-made baits with all kinds of disgusting ingredients. There were stories of fishing with liver, bacon, and chicken, and one guy said he caught his big fish using a McDonalds Quarter Pounder with Cheese. It was good etiquette not to question this and besides it was in an article in a real fishing magazine. The man who claimed this feat was very large in the gut and I suspected if there was a McDonald's Quarter Pounder around it never made it to the hook.

I listened intently when the men started drinking their beer and spinning their fish stories. Normally, children could sit silently and listen but were not to speak. They were also not to tell anyone of the salty language in which the stories were told, especially not mom or their wives.

One evening, after a fishing trip with my uncle, the stories had started. Without knowing it I spoke up and began to ask a question. There was a silence and all eyes turned on me. I did not know what penalty there was for speaking during a fishing story but I bet it was really bad. Instead, after a moment, they all started to laugh. My Uncle said, "Very soon now he will be eleven!" Again they all laughed and answered my questions as long as they were about fishing and not about the truth of the stories being told. That would not be fisherman's etiquette after all. In group thinking it was akin to cramming for a math test at school, which of course it was, but more important. I would run home after these sessions and write down all I had learned in my fishing ledger. If they drank too much I figured that they might accidentally be telling some of their fisherman secrets and I wanted to remember each one. Fishing was hard work!

Most of the fishing stories were not related to one common thing but a variety of events, some funny, some serious, some sad and some even with a moral to the story. Most were told over and over and everyone always acted like they had never heard the story before. Then they would laugh and heartily debate, poke fun or give sympathy if it was a particularly sad story. There was however one type of story that was on every man's inventory of fishing stories. It wasn't just a story but adventures they had had with a single fish. He was the biggest ever seen and the hardest ever to catch. He seemed to be possessed with super powers and intelligence. The older boys and the men each had their own versions that grew with each telling. The fish gained its own celebrity status and personality. A fish storyteller was nothing without a story about a run in with this fish in his storybook. For the most part he was a shadow in the water taking baits, snapping fishing lines, making off with expensive lures and there was even a story of him coming out of the water and biting an expensive fishing pole in to two pieces to make his escape. Other versions had him rocking and capsizing boats. I think maybe that some of these versions were used to explain the men who capsized their own boats after drinking a bit too much. It sounded much better if the fish did it. The fish had capsized one fisherman with a big belly and a bigger thirst, six times to date. He lost three motors and two boats. He didn't get to fish for a while because he had to go to a place called "Rehab." The men explained that because of all of his run-ins with this fish he had developed a fear of fishing. Sort of like the soldiers in the old movies who had what they called 'shell shock'. It was very sad. They had named the fish also. His name was Dillinger. I didn't know who Dillinger was so they told me he was an old-time bank robber that could break out of any jail and kept robbing banks. They said they named the fish Dillinger because he could escape any fisherman and kept robbing them of expensive lures, poles and even boats and motors. In the end, they had caught the real Dillinger but it took all of the policemen, FBI G men and others to bring him down. They did not think that this Dillinger would ever be caught though. These stories always brought much emotion and debate and added a common mission to all fishermen. It was the purpose for them to all gather and to try to bring Dillinger in to justice just like the police and the FBI G men. Dillinger in his own way was the ultimate prize and once claimed could bring much fame to the fisherman who finally caught him. On the other hand, the anticipation of Dillinger being out there was what put the fire into the fishermen to get to the water and drop a line as early and as often as possible.

Time marches on. It is now June 18th, two days before my birthday. I was hanging out more and more around the bait shop. I let it be known that on my birthday I would be fishing solo. I kind of let it slip that the world of fishing would be forever changed after that. That was like ringing the dinner bell to a fish dinner in the bait shop. The place went quiet. Stories stopped in mid-telling, the cashier stopped ringing up sales and slowly all eyes turned to me. The man behind the counter said "Oh! How so?" Everyone was waiting for me to speak and change the fishing world but I could not think of anything to say so I said, "That is a fisherman's secret! Fishermen don't tell their secrets!" There was a hum in the room and packets of laughter. One of the older boys yelled, "If that don't beat all! He ain't even soloed yet and has secrets. That will all change if two days from now he don't catch a blamed thing!" Then everyone laughed. I ran out the door and ran all the way home up the stairs to my room and slammed the door. I crawled under my bed in the dark. I did my best thinking there.

I had thought of everything; equipment, place, baits, lures, practicing my skills, studying at the library... But had I really thought of everything? No! I hadn't. I hadn't thought of failure, disgrace, bad weather or just plain bad luck! I sat and evaluated the possibilities and for the first time I felt fear and a dread of the fishing trip in just two days. I slept badly that night. I dreamed I was on the shore fishing. All of the fish had gathered around. Their heads were sticking out of the water and they were all laughing at me and spitting streams of water from their mouths at me like a squirt gun until I had to run away. I woke up in a sweat. I weighed all of the options: the good ones, the not so good ones, and the disasters. How could I face a failure after being so sure the day before? I had to face this like my father and uncle and their fathers before them had done on their own fishing trips. The fear of failure and humiliation to my family and myself still lingered. Once the failure seed was planted it grew like Jack and the Magical Beanstalk overnight. By morning I could not face the trip.

My father and uncle were at the breakfast table with their coffee. They looked at me when I came in and sat down. My uncle said "Son! You look terrible! Are you sick?" Instantly the opportunity arose to cancel the trip. Mom came running and felt my head and asked all those motherly medical questions to which I answered yes to each one of them. She rushed me back to bed after determining undoubtedly an illness was upon me.

I waited for all to leave me to rest and said to myself "Whew! This just might work and it was all my uncle's idea…sort of!"

All through the day I had visitors. The normal mission of these visits was to see how I was feeling and the bringing of the chicken soup, popsicles, ice cream and pop to aid my recovery. I propped up in front of the TV watching cartoons and movies. None of my choices of channels included fishing lest I remind myself of my current predicament. In the evening, mom made all of my favorite foods but I could only eat a little of each of them even though I wanted more so it would prove to them that I was still sick. Then it was off to bed for a good sleep. Sleep was different than awake. For one thing, dreams came and I couldn't switch the channel. This time the fish looked like all of the people at the bait shop. There were also fish that looked like my uncle and father and my father's father. They were all laughing at me and then one loud booming laugh drowned all of the others out. It was Dillinger. He said "So, quitting before you even start! You are not worthy to drop a line to try to catch me! You should be ashamed, ashamed…."

I awoke to voices in the hallway. It was my Dad and my uncle. My uncle was saying, "It is a shame he will have to miss his fishing trip! What a time to get sick!"

Father said it was a shame and then added, "Maybe he isn't quite ready yet anyway. I have noticed signs that maybe fishing is not his first love anymore!" Then they walked on down the hallway for coffee in the kitchen. I sat up! What did my father mean I wasn't ready yet! I had been ready for a long time. It's just that I didn't want to embarrass him if I failed. I did not enjoy the rest of my day!

In the evening my uncle came into my room to visit. He said, "Let me tell you my story of when I was eleven on my first trip. Not the story you have heard up till now---the true story. I didn't do anything to get ready. I was cocky enough to think I already knew all there was to know about fishing. I set my alarm for five AM, but when it went off I hit the snooze button three times until finally I heard people starting to stir in the house. I got up real quick and snuck to the garage so no one would see me and know that I had overslept. I gathered my equipment and ran off through the field before anyone would notice. I didn't think I would have any trouble finding my spot but I went the wrong direction and came out at the wrong place. It took me almost two hours to get my bearings and find the fishing hole that I wanted. I reached for my worms and found that I had left them behind in my rush from the garage. I didn't want to go back so I grabbed a sharp stone and started to dig. I was hot and muddy and I only found three worms for my efforts. I baited my hook and tossed my first cast around lunchtime. I had also forgotten to bring my lunch so now I was hot, muddy and starved. The fish made nibbles at my bait but no real takers. In a short time the three worms were gone with no results on my stringer. I heard a rustle in the bushes and there were two fishermen hiking out of the woods with their catch. They said, "How's the fishing?"

I said "Not so good and I lost my bait!"

They looked at each other and said "Well, you are in luck, we just happen to have some extra worms that will just go to waste!" They gave me their leftovers and my day was able to continue. Without that bit of luck my first day was done before I even got to make a decent try at it.

After several hours I had caught two measly fish. I built a fire and started cleaning them. My knife was dull and I didn't get much meat from what little meat was on these small fish. As I got out my skillet I dropped the fish in the dirt. I put the oil in the skillet and placed it on the fire and went to the creek to wash the dirt off of my fish. I had built the fire too big and the grease got too hot.

When I threw the wet fish pieces into the grease it popped loudly and shot grease everywhere. As the grease landed in the fire it ignited and shot big flames up and ignited the grease in the frying pan. It was all too hot to grab the pan so I grabbed a big stick and pushed the pan out of the raging fire. While doing this, the pan tipped and the flaming grease spilled into the leaves around the site and then began to burn. I grabbed water from the creek several times but it made it worse. I finally wet the leaves and area around the fire and let it burn out and stomped it out with my feet when I could. I had almost started a forest fire. I had dodged another potential disaster on my first trip. Finally I looked in the pan and found four small cinders that used to be my fish dinner. I ate the fish cinders anyway and almost threw up and felt kind of ill for a while after that. Finally, I decided to take one more try. I took my Pole and let it go way back. I let it fly with all of my might. The rig flew over my head and made a perfect cast with my arching line heading straight for a downed tree laying in the water. It was a huge tree and the branches now reached skyward like dark hands trying to catch my line. I prayed silently it would clear the tree and then I could just walk down past the tree and reel it in.

I should have known with the way this day was going that prayer was the only hope. This did not happen. The line landed smack dab into the middle of the tree. I slowly pulled at it. No good! I gave it a yank! Again, No good!

I started yelling and swearing and yanking and pulling and making myself look like I was in a sword fight with an imaginary enemy. I was aware that I looked very silly and looked around to see if anyone was watching. Finally, I walked to the tree. The limbs were so thick I couldn't get anywhere near the tangled line or hook to free it. I had to cut my line. While doing this I dropped my bait into the water and it swiftly floated downstream to the delight of the fish in the area. I went home dejected. I told my dad that I caught two big fish and ate them both and couldn't eat another bite. I went to my room hungry! Many years later I can laugh about this failure and my comical day of fishing. I could also see that no matter what happened that day my dad would be proud, my family would continue to love me and a new day would rise each morning. I could not let this one fishing trip affect my life in a big way. There would be many more fishing trips that would go better. The event was really nothing more than one small star in a sky filled with billions, maybe trillions, of radiant stars and no one except me would notice.

Anyway, I had other bites. I cleaned and cooked the catch. I told him it really didn't matter because whatever story I told them would be accepted for what it was worth. That was fishing etiquette. I hope you remember that this trip is for fun and won't change you or those around you in the end." With that he stood and told me to feel better and left. I heard his footsteps down the hallway and the front screen door squeak and slam shut. His pick-up truck engine fired and I could hear the crunch of gravel under his tires as he pulled away down the drive as he left. I had an odd feeling of peace and a new resolve to make my trip in the morning. I set my alarm for 5 AM.

The alarm went off. It seemed very early and it was. I gathered my gear, brushed my teeth and hair, got dressed and headed to the kitchen and joined my mother, father and uncle. They all looked surprised. My mother said, "You feel all right? You are sick!" and felt my head. Father said, "Leave the boy alone dear. It appears he has made a recovery!" She said, "I know about boy's illnesses! It is a mother's duty! If you insist on letting him go then I insist that his brother go with him!" My father and uncle looked at each other baffled. I stared in horror and broke in and said "No! He will be mad if you make him go and this is my trip. I will have coffee mother!" I looked at my father's and uncle's cups and added, "I take it black!" They all smiled---except mother. I secretly knew that if my brother was called upon, I would have a beating coming from him and the whole day would be teasing, pranks and undertakings to ruin the trip. My mother brought the coffee. I took a sip---ugh--I never tasted black coffee before! I finished it anyway and ate my breakfast and exited the door to a chorus of good lucks and just one shout of "Have fun!" from my uncle.

As I walked down the drive I heard the screen door slam behind me. My father and uncle called me over to the pick-up truck. Father said "Big day son! You will do fine! On a fishing trip you have to go with whatever happens. Some days are good, some aren't so good and others are just plain disasters. But they are all fishing days and God has given us nothing better in my estimation! Do your best and I will be proud of you no matter how it turns out!"

He nodded to my uncle who opened the truck door and pulled out the most beautiful fishing pole I ever laid eyes on. He said, "Your father and I decided that a boy your age should have a fishing pole that a fisherman would be proud to own. This pole is for you for good luck!"

I looked at it and held it and flipped it around.

It was a fine pole. I felt a tear in my eye but I could not let it escape in front of them. I said "Thank you! I appreciate it!" and started my two mile walk to my chosen spot.

It is always cool in the mornings at this early time of day and I felt the chill. I opted not to wear a coat because in a short time it would just be extra baggage. My talk with my uncle had given me a sense of peace. My father's words rang in my ears and gave me purpose. No longer was it important to have a TV show or millions of dollars and fame. It was only important to stay true to myself and to give my best effort based on my skills, brains, and some measure of luck. While in these thoughts I made my way down the trail and could hear the gurgling, splashing water of the stream. The morning dew had dampened my shoes and legs and the ground was still wet. The rising sun that would dry up the dew now only made it sparkle like a thousand small lights. The clearing opened up on the water and this same morning light made the water glisten with white and orange sparkles. The sight of the water with its hidden treasures and adventures always for a moment took my breath away. I stood and surveyed the scene and felt a new feeling of growth and fulfillment. I knew that after this trip things in my life would never be the same. Now that this journey had begun it was like a door to my past childhood had slammed shut and that which came before placed forever in memories. I had read in a magazine that sharks must continually swim forward. They cannot stop or go backwards or they will die. This compared to my current feelings and I boldly moved forward.

I located my spot that I had scouted out. I had spent time building quite an encampment here in preparations for this day. It included a cleaning station, fire pit made out of river rock, tree stump chairs and a large supply of firewood and kindling to last for a while. This was my base of operations. I even had a lean-to shelter built here. I sat down and unpacked my gear. The sun was still glowing orange and the first yellow rays were appearing. The shadows in the woods and along the shoreline were changing from blacks and grays to greens and browns and other vibrant colors. The animals were waking and starting to scurry around shouting orders in various animal languages to each other. A deer came to the water a short distance away to drink. Of more interest were the coatings of water bugs floating on the currents and the splashing of the fish as they surfaced open mouthed to collect them for their morning meals. They would then flip over and dive down into the dark water and make another try. This was a good sign for a fisherman and promised that the day would be a good one. This was precisely why I had chosen this spot. I readied my poles and baited my hooks and moved to the water for my first cast.

I threw out the line on my old pole first because if felt comfortable and I was used to it. The cast landed right where I planned. The bobber surfaced and floated on the current. I then cast out my new pole. It felt lighter and the reel more precise and solid. The cast button was easy to use. I choose a spot so the lines would not tangle with each other and threw the cast. It sailed and sailed and made a resounding plop far out in the water. It went much further than I was used to with my other pole. I set the drag and made a pole holder out of rocks and sticks to hold both poles while they tempted the fish below with my bait. I started to put wood in the fire pit to build a fire. I noticed the tip of the new pole starting to bounce. Something was nibbling on the current out in the stream. Just as fast now I heard the drag make its noise. I threw down the wood and ran for the pole. To my astonishment the pole leaped from the pole holder and was making its escape towards the water. I ran for it and dove and caught it just as it cleared the bank. I could feel the hook set and then the strong pull of a fish on the other end of the line trying to gain its freedom. I reeled in the slack and kept pressure on the line. I pulled on the pole to ease the fish towards me and then quickly took up the slack once more. This process would be repeated several times. Sometimes the fish gained ground and sometimes I gained ground. The battle for life and death had begun. I knew it would be a battle of patience. As soon as I had this thought something appeared on the water just out of my vision. A large log was drifting on the water and could come into the battle if I could not get the fish clear of its path before it reached my line in the water. It would surely snag the line and snap it off. I would have to cut the line to save my pole. I pulled and reeled--pulled and reeled--- pulled and reeled as hard as I dared. I was lucky that the fish had chosen my new pole to bite on because the line on it was much heavier and less likely to break. The log had picked up speed on the current and was bearing down on the battle. Sweat poured off of my forehead stinging my eyes but I held on---the distance shortening every second and I was not yet clear of the hazard. It appeared that I would not make it. With one mighty heave I fell backwards reeling like a madman. The log touched the line and tried to hold on to it to my horror. The pole jumped in my hands but I held tight---my knife ready to cut the line if necessary. Suddenly there was a quick slackening of the line and I watched it pop loose from the log and bounce into the water as the tree passed by and moved away. I thought I had lost my fish and started to reel in the line. At once it went taught and I again felt the line under heavy weight. I continued to pull and reel. As the line reached about twenty feet I got my first glimpse of my prize. It was a large mouthed bass of very good size jumping up and splashing back down to dive out of the hook. I kept the pressure on and pulled and reeled and pulled and reeled. I could feel the fish beginning to tire. In a few more minutes I had him to shore and led him into my net. I raised it in triumph and knew that my fear of disgrace was no longer a problem. The fish was probably 1 1/2 to 2 pounds and would make my first solo meal all by itself. I put him on my stringer and took my pliers out and removed the hook. I placed him in my catch bucket and lowered it back into the stream water. The catch bucket had holes in it so the water would flow through and keep my catch alive but not let him escape until I would eat him or take him home. I had no sooner put him back in the water when my old pole came to life. The bobber in the water moved up and down like a piston. I grabbed the pole and reeled it in. It was much easier and told me the fish was not as big as the one I just landed. It was a very lively fish and was giving me all that it had. I netted it and began to laugh. I remembered my uncle's story of his first trip and this fish would have probably been smaller than the ones that he had caught on that fateful day and I certainly had no appetite for cinder fish. I unhooked the fish and put him back in the water to grow for another day. The pressure of the day was now broken. I was excited and wanted to run to tell my uncle and father but the day promised to be a perfect fishing day and I knew I had to stay.

By lunchtime, I had hooked and landed ten additional good-sized fish. I had caught and released another ten smaller ones. It was time for a break and lunch. I took my first catch from the bucket and laid him out on the cleaning rock I had made. I took my fishing knife out and sliced the length of its stomach and opened it up to remove the insides and put them aside. I then made two cuts down the top bone and slid the knife in first one side and then the other side. On each side I found the rib bones and sliced the meat away from the bone making very nice and thick fillets. Once the meat was stripped, I placed the carcass aside. I would later place it out to be discovered by the wildlife and share the feast with them. I had the fire going and washed the fillets with my bottled water. I coated them with oil and put oil in the skillet to heat and put the pan back on the fire. There is a test to see the oil is ready. You simply put a drop of water on it and it if sizzles it is time to cook. I took out my coating bag and put in the fish pieces and shook it to coat them evenly. The bag was filled with corn meal, flour, salt, pepper and paprika. I put a drop of water in the pan and it popped and sizzled like it was supposed to and told me I was ready to cook. I took the battered fish from the bag and laid them in the grease. I opened a jar that contained French fried potatoes that I had cut up at home and kept in water so they wouldn't turn brown and also put them in the grease. I took my camping plate and silverware from my pack and put them on my rock table that I had built and pulled up my tree stump chair. The fish and fries sizzled and filled the air with wonderful smells. I got in my cooler and pulled out a coke. I flipped the fish and stirred the fries so they browned on all sides. In the bushes I heard a rustle. I thought it was probably an animal drawn by the smell of the cooking food. I picked up the remains of the fish and tossed it in the direction of the noise. The rustling stopped and I sat down to have probably the best meal of my life. I had caught, cleaned and cooked it by myself and that would make it taste all that much better. I finished my meal and threw the scraps into the bushes for the animals. I washed my skillet and camp plate and stowed them away. I would clean them better later at home. I was full and happy and knew this would be a good day. My luck continued and I caught five more fish for my stringer. The rest of the catch would be catch-and-release for the day so as not to deplete the amount of fish in the river. About mid-afternoon I took a nap!

I dozed for a while and again was visited by dreams. The fish were all there staring at me. They were not laughing anymore but just staring at me. There was a gurgling sound in the water and then a big splash. The big whiskered face of Dillinger was pushed very close to my face. He said, "So you do have the guts but you have not caught me yet!" With that he faded back under the water laughing loudly and disappeared into the dark depths. I awoke in a sweat. It had been a successful day but it would be too much to hope for to catch Dillinger on my solo trip. No one would believe it if I did catch him. I sat quietly and thought for a while. Catching Dillinger would stop all the laughing for sure. But once this fish was taken would all other fish be second best or would another fish just take his place. I again heard rustling in the bushes but had nothing left to throw. It was late afternoon now and I considered calling it a day--a very successful day at that. I decided to rig the new pole for bottom fishing, and make a couple of casts for Dillinger and then go home with my catch and my new fishing stories. I threw the line out far to the deep channel in the middle of the creek and it made a satisfying plunk and the bobber floated on the current. It followed the current downstream with no results. I reeled it in and recast five times with similar results. I decided I would try one more time but expected the same outcome. I leaned way back and let the rig fly. It arched far out into the water. It was much farther than my other casts of the day. I heard the familiar Ker-plunk as it hit deep water and quickly reeled in the slack and set the drag.

I was surprised to hear a second large splash and looked up to see a gigantic tail fin headed back under. The waves radiated outward like a tsunami and swamped my feet when they reached the bank. I felt my line go taught and tightened my grip just in time before the pole was ripped from my hands. The pole bent almost double and the drag-line whistled as the fish ran with it. Finally this initial hit subsided and the line went slack. I thought I had lost my fish and quickly reeled the line in to make another cast.

The line remained slack. As the bobber lay about twenty feet out a large dark body knifed through the water and rose between the bobber and where I stood and splashed back down sideways sending a wave of water in my direction that soaked my clothes to the skin. I shivered and held on and kept reeling. There was a ripple in the water. I saw a vision of a submarine surfacing but it was the head of the fish coming right back at me. He abruptly stopped and peered at me standing there drenched and shivering and a sort of smile appeared on his face. He turned and slapped his tail hard and sent another sheet of water my way with the same drenching affect. The line once again tensioned and the drag was singing away. My glimpse of the fish told me he was bigger than either my father or uncle by size comparison. He was huge! I held on tight! I again heard rustling in the bushes and thought the whole forest was coming to watch this battle play out. This running in and out on the line continued for a long time. A normal fish would have tired by now and been in my net. This one still seemed to be toying with me. So be it! My hook was set deep and my equipment was in good shape. My mind was focused to the task but I was starting to feel weary. I hoped he was too! This fish was smart. He looked for every advantage but there was nothing now to be had except a battle of endurance between a fisherman and a fish. It is the way it should be and has been since the beginning of time when men caught fish for their very existence. I pictured the cavemen catching fish by hand and ran through history and various types of fishing. My mind wandered a little here. I was brought back to reality by a stiff jerk on the pole. One of my hands fell away but the other still gripped solidly. I recovered quickly and grabbed the pole above the real to get control. My hand was over the line. I heard the sound of the drag playing out and the line was going out fast. It bit into my hand and brought blood instantly. I pulled my hand quickly and got it back on the reel. I had passed his current test and still had him on the line. My hand was throbbing and blood ran down my arm.

I heard a low rumble and glanced to the sky. I saw a flash of lightning and saw dark angry clouds rolling in towards my position. I stayed planted and focused on my fish. The storm was moving quickly. We were at a stalemate, each waiting to see what the other would do. The attacks by the fish had stopped. I kept the line taught but was not reeling and pulling the line. We both seemed to be watching as the incoming storm moved towards us.

The wind was picking up. Leaves and debris

were sucked off the ground and pulled airborne. The lightning and thunder was becoming intense. The rumble of thunder now turned to sharp cracks. Lightning flooded the sky with electric fingers creeping through black clouds. There was a very bright light and a loud boom. My body tingled and my hair stood on end. There was a smell and feel of electricity in the air. In science class we know this was called ozone.

The wind was becoming stronger. The sky was now a greenish gray. A large tree by the bend into the inlet where I sat was leaning precariously over the water. Where its trunk split there were splinters of smoking wood and bright glowing embers from a recent lightning strike. The wind was now very strong and the cloud was moving in a slow and ominous circle. I tightened my grip on the pole. The animals had all deserted now to find shelter. Rain was pelting down in cold sheets. Shortly it was followed by a hailstorm. At first the hail was the size of a pea but increased to the size of golf balls quickly. They struck and stung my body but it quickly passed. Through the thunder there now arose a noise. A loud clacking, rumbling noise moving through the trees on the opposite shoreline. There was a lot of debris in the air. I could see trees bending low now and some flying through the air. There was a path of destruction through the trees like a giant prehistoric beast was taking them down in an angry fit. The creek quickly became swollen and filled with debris. The sound intensified along with the rain and lightning. The thunder was drowned out by the sound of the storm upon me. I wanted to cover my ears but instead I crawled to the big rock in the encampment and braced myself against the wind with a death grip on my pole. My line was slack but I reeled it in and again found the tension.

The fish had retreated into my inlet to avoid the debris floating in the channel. It was instinctive for the fish to find shelter. I was in a safe place now. Flood waters naturally drained to the other bank and into the flood plain beyond. The noise finally subsided and the storm moved away. I could see it through the holes in the forest that was now stripped of standing timber as it moved down the plain. I prayed it would not hit my house or anyone else's house; but that was in God's hands. There was still debris falling from the sky. The creek was full of it. Some of the floating pieces looked like roofing off of houses or barns. Then the creek and the woods were overcome by an eerie silence. The gurgle of the water was the only undisturbed sound.

There was a loud creak, then a louder moan

and then a loud crack as the stricken tree lost its battle for survival and tumbled towards the water. Suddenly the pole came to life. The fish and I realized at the same time that the path of the tree would completely block the inlet and any chance of escape. The battle was back on, but I knew, as did the fish, that he had waited too long to react and the tree landed with a loud splash. Quickly, any avenue of escape was sealed as the flotsam of the creek was grabbed by the reaching tree limbs and sealed any possible hole that could be used.

I reeled the line taught but the fish no longer fought and seemed certain of its fate. I crawled up to the water and could see his large mass swimming in circles. Finally, he faced me, and our eyes met. It was not what I had expected. He looked sad and I did not feel the excitement in my victory or even pride. It was to be me against the fish. There could be no interference…not even from God! I did not have a way to net this fish. I did not think I had the strength left to pull him from the water. A fish like this could make me famous but it had not been a fair fight. There could be no pride in it. The fish moved closer. I reached my hand into the water. He came closer and nuzzled my hand under the water like a congratulations.

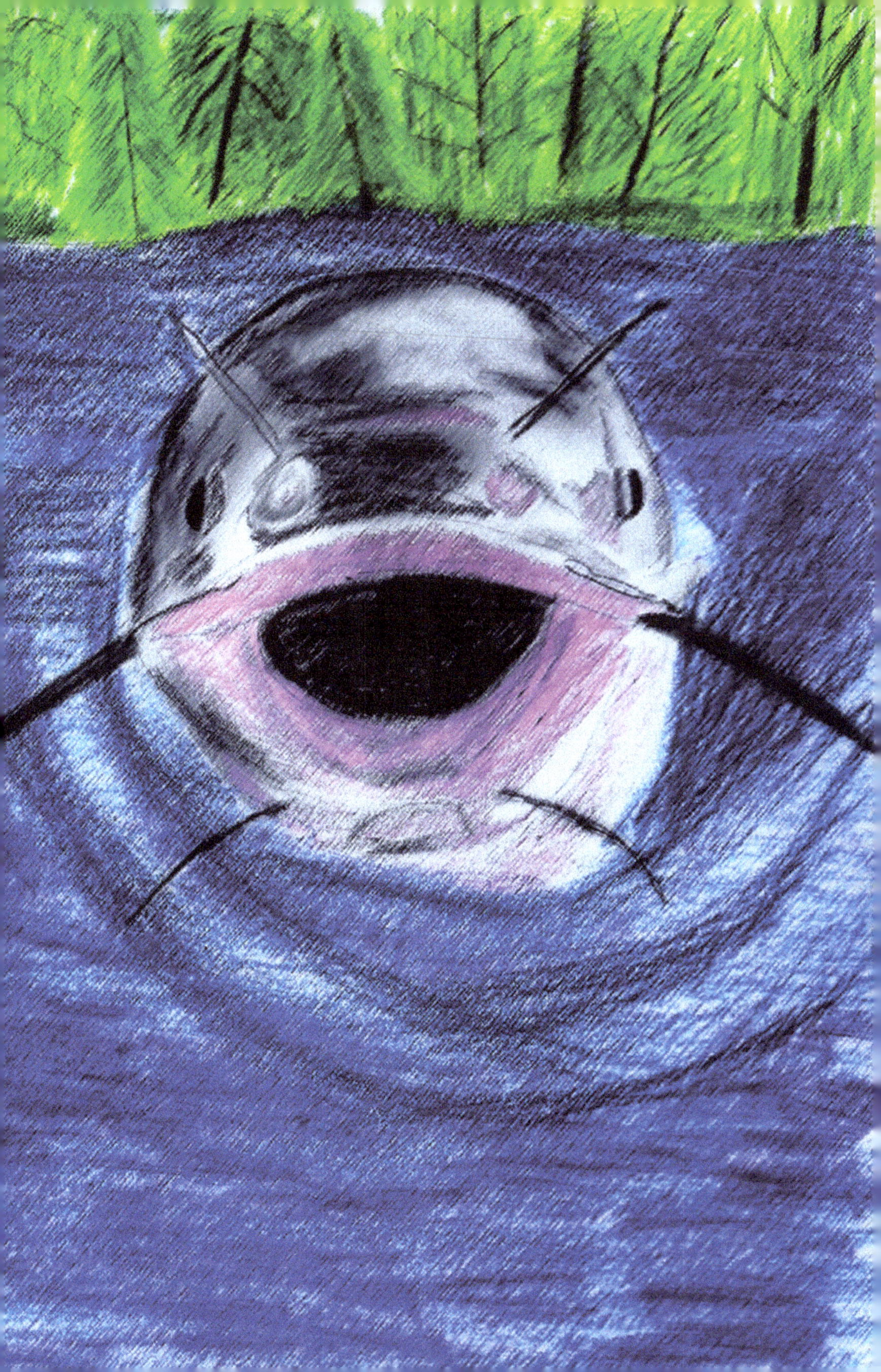

I reached down and removed my hook from his mouth. I waded into the water and took a large limb and poked a hole through the debris. This was no easy task. I had to take my scout hatchet and cut some of the limbs hanging into the water to make a hole big enough in the dam for his escape. Finally the opening was large enough if I held the limb up in place. The fish slowly circled and nudged my leg. His head broke the surface and his smile was back. He dove down through the hole while I held it open. He surfaced past the fallen tree and rolled onto his side. His fin wiggled into the air like a good bye and he disappeared with a large splash of his tail into the deep channel.

I reeled in and stacked my poles and packed my tackle box. I rebuilt the fire to stay warm. Fallen trees and debris blocked the path around me. I knew it was best to stay where I was and let help find me.

I sat by the fire and felt its warmth as it started to dry my shoes and clothes. After a while I could hear chain saws and shouts. I got my knife out and cleaned and filleted three of the fish. I cleared the encampment of its clutter and got my skillet. I put it on the fire to heat up. I heard the shouts of my father and uncle and called back to them. They entered my encampment to the smell of frying fish and sat down by the fire. We hugged like men hug--a quick wrap of the arms and a hard pat on the back. I got out three of the tin plates. We ate our fish in silence and drank a coke. My uncle broke the silence and said "Well! What of your fish story?" We looked at each other and laughed. I pulled up my stringer to show them my catch. I slowly related the day's events but left out my adventure with Dillinger---at least I thought he must have been Dillinger but that too would be speculation throughout my life.

My father patted me on the back and picked up some of my gear. He said "We best be gettin' back. There will be lots of storm work to do!" We stopped by the police station where we always reported in times of crisis!

Several homes had been hit by the storm. Some were damaged to different degrees and a few were just gone. These people were housed in the church nearby. We quickly cleaned my catch and delivered them to the church kitchen to feed these unfortunate people and then worked into the night collecting belongings, clearing debris and cutting up fallen trees to help open streets and restore power.

Over the weeks ahead there would be much more work helping neighbors and making repairs. I did not fish for several weeks during this period.

Finally the work was done and the contractors had moved in to finish rebuilding houses and barns.

I walked to the bait store. It was quite crowded and quite loud as the fishing stories had not been told for many weeks now. As I entered the room went quiet. There was a lot of nudging and pointing. I went to the counter and bought my coke. The cashier winked at the others and said "Don't I recollect that you was soloing the day the storm hit?" I answered yes. He said, "That must be quite a fish story! I think you should tell us!"

I told the story for the first time that day in public. I did not tell the part about Dillinger only that I had a big one on the line when the storm came and he got away. They all laughed and an old man said "Ain't no shame in that--we've all let big ones get away and it seems God had a hand in this one!" I told this story hundreds of times over my life and got pretty good at tellin' it. Some people say that as you grow older the mind fades some. Some even say if you tell the same story over and over again you start to believe the enhancements that you put to it. I will leave that for you to decide about which parts are true and which parts aren't!

My uncle and my father both got older and didn't fish nearly as often. I never got my TV show but did win a few fishing tournaments. I would take my father and uncle to my encampment to fish whenever they would go. The encampment had grown. I had used many logs from the storm to build a fishing cabin on the spot. I also trimmed up the ancient tree that fell that day and carved some seats into its trunk from which to fish. It was on one of these autumn days that we were all perched on that tree with our lines wet that my uncle said "I remember when you were almost eleven. I came to your room and told you the true story of my first fishing trip. I think it is time you told us the whole true story. You see I have never told you but on that day I sat in the woods watching you fish all day. Twice that day you threw fish guts on me in the bushes right over there in my hiding place. They stuck on my hat and hung off my ear---this one right here! I saw it all that day. Tell us your true fishing story! It is much better than the one you normally tell and I think your father should hear it from you!" I sat for a moment and let it all sink in. I shifted in my seat and told the true story of that day as I remembered it to my two best fishing buddies. There was a lot of discussion following the story about the lucky new pole, fishing baits, how weather affects the fish and fishing luck and skill but mostly a silent understanding of the now shared experience. I didn't change my public story and the true story was only told this once until now.

While fishing you often ponder your life as it winds down. My father and uncle had long since passed to the better life. I thought of that day many times. I learned the obvious lessons on fishing, storytelling, equipment, lures, baits, etc., but I learned much, much more. I learned of the soul of nature that exists in every living thing. I learned the lesson of how communities and neighbors pull together in times of crisis to raise each other's spirits and meet each other's needs. I learned the caring and supportive nature of family and friends throughout life. My solo fishing trip had turned out to be much, much more than I could have imagined. I remember my thought that day on the two-mile hike to the encampment that once that trip had begun I could never go back to childhood…and I never did!

So, another fishing story begins.

www.ingramcontent.com/pod-product-compliance
Lightning Source LLC
Chambersburg PA
CBHW061109100726
47911CB00012B/481